Adventures with Sister Philomena,
Special Agent to the Pope

Secrets
of
Siena

Written by DIANNE AHERN

Illustrated by BILL SHURTLIFF

Aunt Dee's Attic, Inc.

Adventures with Sister Philomena,
Special Agent to the Pope:
SECRETS OF SIENA

Copyright 2011 Aunt Dee's Attic, Inc.

A Book from Aunt Dee's Attic

Published by *Aunt Dee's Attic, Inc.*
415 Detroit Street, Suite 200
Ann Arbor, MI 48104

Manufactured in Italy by L.E.G.O. SpA
October 2010

Library of Congress Control Number: 2010936763

ISBN 13: 978-0-9829416-0-7
ISBN 10: 0-9829416-0-9

1 2 3 4 5 6 7 8 9 10

First Edition

www.auntdeesattic.com

This book is dedicated to Riley and Delaney Miner

Special Thank You and Acknowledgments to . . .

. . . the Fil and McManus families for opening their homes and hearts to Dianne and Bill in creation of the artwork for this book,

. . . Father Bill Ashbaugh, Pastor of St. Thomas the Apostle Catholic Church, Ann Arbor, and for his review of this manuscript with respect to Church teachings,

. . . the proofreaders, editors, and reviewers who came to the aid of the author, including: Lisa Renee Tucci, Josiah Shurtliff, Shiobhan Kelly, Leo DiGiulio, and LeAnn Fields,

. . . Jillian Downey for the work on the text layout and design.

Other books by Dianne Ahern:

BOOKS ON THE SACRAMENTS:
Today I Was Baptized
Today I Made My First Reconciliation
Today I Made My First Communion
Today Someone I Love Passed Away
Today We Became Engaged

ADVENTURES WITH SISTER PHILOMENA,
SPECIAL AGENT TO THE POPE SERIES:
Book 1: *Lost in Peter's Tomb*
Book 2: *Break-in at the Basilica*
Book 3: *Curse of the Coins*

CHAPTER ONE

GOING ON HOLIDAY

"Children, where are you?" Sister Philomena cries excitedly as she rushes out of Mother Superior's office. She has some wonderful news to share with Riley and Delaney. Looking over the stone wall that surrounds the convent, she spots her young nephew, Riley, playing soccer with some boys who live nearby. Sister Philomena thinks Riley is an incredible boy. Despite the fact that he came to Italy not being able to speak a word of Italian, he has made friends with the local boys and they are learning each others' languages.

"Riley, *vieni qui,* come here," sings out Sister Philomena, "I have something to tell you. Where's your sister?"

Immediately Riley suspects that the Pope has called upon his aunt to tackle another special assignment. These often involve an investigation or a mystery surrounding the Church, and she often lets Riley and his sister Delaney accompany her. The thought of being able to participate in another of Aunt Philomena's special assignments takes Riley's focus off the game. In

1

that second, one of the boys on the opposing team kicks the soccer ball right past Riley and into the goal.

"*Gooooal,*" the boy kicking the ball shouts in Italian. "*BASTA!* Game over! We win." Riley looks at his teammates and is about to apologize for missing the block when they all start laughing. "Time to go pray, *Americano,*" they tease in a joking and friendly way. The other players respect Riley as a good player and a fair person, and realize that it was not his choice to be staying at the convent, but something his family arranged.

"Win some, lose some!" the boys cheer. "*Ciao, ciao.*"

"We must find Delaney," Sister Philomena urges, as Riley runs up the hill to meet her. "I have a surprise and a treat for all of us."

"She's in the kitchen with Sister Adelaide," Riley responds. "Did the Pope call you with an assignment?"

"No, even better. I'll explain when we find Delaney."

Delaney and Riley have been staying with their aunt in the guest quarters of her convent in Grottaferrata, Italy, since the beginning of the summer. The children's parents had business to conduct in Southern France and Northern Italy over the summer, and rather than leaving their children at home with a nanny, decided it would be great for them to spend the summer in Italy with their aunt, the nun. But of course their parents had no idea that, besides being a nun, Sister Philomena was also a secret investigative agent for the Pope.

When he first got there, Riley had major issues about living in a convent full of nuns. He thought that all that nuns did was go to church and pray—day-in and day-out. He was so sure that he would die of boredom, not to mention embarrassment, that he made plans to run away. But he had a major change of attitude after experiencing what his aunt's life is really like. It's awesome to be here, and he wouldn't trade this summer for anything.

The nuns have warmly accepted Delaney and Riley as welcome guests and members of their community. Mother Superior has been wonderfully surprised by how well the children have fit into the flow of activity at the convent. Riley is quick to help out with the chores. Because he is growing up on a farm back home, he knows all about farm animals and gardening. He eagerly helps care for the animals that the nuns keep on the convent grounds—cows and goats for milk and cheese, and chickens for eggs. He also gets up early in the morning, before the sun gets too hot, to weed the garden and walk the grape arbors looking for insect pests. Riley thinks it's funny that these nuns use the grapes they grow to make wine—

lots of it. It must be pretty good wine, as it is used by the Vatican and several churches in Rome for consecration during Masses. Over the summer Riley has gained a sense of pride in the work of the convent.

Delaney is a few years younger than Riley and is just learning to read. She loves to draw pictures and says she wants to be an artist when she grows up. Aunt Philomena has taken her to places all over Italy where she could see pictures of every kind, many of them painted right on the walls! Like her older brother, Delaney seems to have an ear for languages and is really fast at picking up Italian words and phrases.

The young girl has become a good friend of Sister Adelaide, the nun in charge of the convent's kitchen and meals. If Delaney isn't sitting at one of the huge dining room tables drawing pictures, she can be found in the kitchen trying to help Sister Adelaide prepare meals.

As Riley suspected, they find Delaney in the kitchen sitting on her favorite stool right beside Sister Adelaide. It's funny to see the old nun and little girl chatting and gesturing excitedly as they prepare food for the evening meal.

"Like this?" questions Delaney as she carefully takes a chunk of potato mixture from a bowl, rolls it into a ball, and then squishes it with a fork. You can see the fork imprints she made all over the potato

mixture. They're making *gnocchi*, a type of small potato dumpling cooked in boiling water and then mixed with tomato sauce or a creamy cheese sauce and served instead of spaghetti.

"*Perfetto*," praises Sister Adelaide, then continues jabbering on in Italian. Although she doesn't speak much English and Delaney doesn't know a lot of Italian, the two seem to understand each other perfectly.

"Children, Mother Superior has given me permission to take you two on a holiday! I am so excited! We're going to Siena for the *Palio*!" announces Sister Philomena. "The family of one of the sisters in our convent has an apartment right above the main Piazza del Campo in Siena—and that gives us a ringside seat at the famous horse race, called the Palio."

Riley and Delaney look at each other quizzically.

"I'm telling you, the Palio is one of the biggest and most exciting events in all of Italy. It happens twice a year, once in July and again in August. It's a stupendous horse race that takes place right in the middle of the town, in their main *piazza*. The days before the race are filled with festivals, celebrations, and special blessings. People spend all year preparing for the festival and bragging about their favorite teams. It's just plain awesome!"

"Where is Siena?" questions Riley.

"It's about three or four hours north of Rome—just a little south of Florence," explains Sister Philomena.

"How will we get there?" asks Riley. He's hoping they will be able to travel there in the Pope's private car. Then he realizes that won't happen because they're going on their own holiday, not a papal assignment.

"Well, I suppose I could borrow the convent's car and drive us," says Sister Philomena. Riley cringes at the thought. Sister Philomena pretends to ignore the pained expression on his face. "However," she continues while giving Riley the 'evil eye', "the driving and parking in Siena will be next to impossible with the crowds there for the Palio. So I guess that means we take the train. Is that OK with you?"

"Cool!" sing out Riley and Delaney. "We love taking the train. When do we leave?"

"We will leave in the morning and be gone for about a week," smiles Sister Philomena. "*Andiamo*, let's go pack our things. This is so exciting! We're going to Siena on holiday!"

SIENA

The trip by train from Rome to Siena is as exciting for Riley and Delaney as was their first train ride in Italy. The scenery is full of wonder—there are fields of sunflowers for miles and miles, rolling hills filled with row upon row of grape arbors, groves of olive trees and fruit trees, herds of sheep being watched over by sheepdogs, and small villages with rows of houses whose gardens back right up to the railroad tracks.

"That field doesn't look right. Shouldn't there be something growing there?" asks Delaney. In the distance she sees rolling hills consisting of nothing but big clumps of gray dirt. Delaney turns to her aunt for an explanation.

"It does look out of place in this very green countryside," muses Sister Philomena. "But that gray dirt is actually clay soil used to make pottery—dishes, cups, vases, all kinds of things. The earth is full of gifts!"

It is late afternoon by the time they get off the train in Siena. Sister Philomena has the porter drop their bags on the curb outside the train station, then turns to Riley and Delaney, "Here's the taxi stand. You two stay here, and if a taxi comes, open its door and make the taxi driver wait for us. Tell him, *'aspetta, per favore'*. That means 'please wait'. I'm going over there to get some money from the cash machine."

Riley and Delaney stand watch over the bags and wait patiently for a taxi to arrive.

"Look at them," Delaney says to Riley in a loud whisper as she points to a couple standing nearby. She has been watching a man and woman in front of the train station, waving their arms, talking loudly in Italian, and generally creating a scene. "She's scolding him! See how she shakes her finger at him. Boy, he must be in big trouble. I wonder what he did."

"Oh, oh. She just called him *'idiota'*, and I am pretty sure that means *idiot*," snickers Riley in a hushed voice.

The children continue to watch as the man and woman carry on. The next thing that Riley understands them saying is *la lettera*. He thinks that means *letter* in Italian. The man shrugs his shoulders as if to say, "I don't know." Now the woman seems really mad. The man pulls a piece of paper from his pocket, unfolds it, and shows it to the woman. *"La carta! La mia carta!"* shouts the man. He's nearly in tears and tries to explain something to the woman. Riley knows

that *la carta* can mean either *paper* or *map* in Italian. The paper looks like it has something scribbled on it—it could be a hand-drawn map. The woman looks at the paper, and then gives the man a hug—he hugs her back and they dance around in place. They must be friends again!

"Taxi?" A man's voice interrupts.

Riley turns to see a taxi driver standing next to him and offering to put their bags in the taxi's trunk.

"*Si, signore*. Yes, sir," Riley answers, "*aspetta, per favore,*" he remembers to say, asking the driver to wait for a moment. "Delaney, go tell Aunt Philomena that the taxi is here."

Riley and Delaney are all eyes as the taxi approaches the centuries-old wall that surrounds the old part of Siena. The red brick and stone wall looms way above their heads. Riley has learned that walls like this were built around Italian towns hundreds and hundreds of years ago to protect the townspeople from outside invaders. In the walls are huge openings every so often, gateways that allow traffic to pass into and out of the cities. A long time ago, these gateways would have been guarded by local armies or officials who would have stopped travelers to collect tolls or taxes, but you don't have to pay to enter the city now.

There is a huge sense of excitement in the air, as bright colorful flags fly from every doorway and window, people jam the streets, laughter and singing fill the air—the place is alive! Their hearts begin to beat fast.

The taxi makes its way through the narrow, crowded streets of Siena, then comes to an abrupt stop in the middle of a street in front of a multi-storied red brick building. The sign in front reads *Palazzo Vincenti*.

"*Palazzo*? Doesn't that mean *palace* in Italian?" asks Riley. "Are we staying in a palace?" He cannot imagine this to be true.

"As a matter of fact, we are," says Sister Philomena. "At least it was a palace hundreds of years ago. The Vincenti family has owned this *palazzo* forever. The family's living quarters where we will be staying are on the upper floors, their offices are on the second floor, and a first floor is rented out for shops and a restaurant. Now, in reality it's a palace in name only."

Sister Philomena checks to make sure the children look presentable after their long train ride, then presses what looks like a doorbell button below the sign and to the right of an iron gate. After a few seconds a buzzer sounds and the gate swings open automatically. In front of them is a pair of huge bronze doors. They're so big that a pair of horse and riders could

probably pass through them. The bronze doors creak as they slowly part. Sister Philomena and the children pick up their bags and cautiously enter.

Riley and Delaney find themselves standing in the center of a large, dimly lit entry hall. The ceiling is so high and so dark, it is out of sight. As their eyes adjust to the darkness, they see a marble staircase in front of them. The only light is from candles and torches. The stair steps slope to the center as if they have been worn down from hundreds, maybe even thousands, of

years of use. Despite the summer heat outside, it's cool and damp inside. It smells musty, like a haunted house would smell. Riley looks at his sister. Her eyes are big and dark and scared looking, and he feels a chill.

"Drop 'em there," a booming male voice with a strong Italian accent echoes through the hall. Riley and Delaney look around to try and find the voice, but it's too dark to see anyone. The children drop their bags and take a step closer to their aunt.

Suddenly a man dressed like a jester in a gold and red striped shirt with puffy sleeves, striped leggings, and a four-cornered hat emerges from the darkness. "*Buona sera!*" the man's voice booms. "I take care of your bags." The strangely dressed man grabs their luggage and disappears into the darkness.

"This place is spooky," Riley thinks out loud. "It feels like we're taking a giant step back in time. In fact, I wouldn't be surprised if I ran into someone in a suit of armor in a place like this." Riley steps away from his aunt to get a better look at things. As he backs up, he trips. Something catches him—something cold to the touch and with metal arms! As he scrambles to his feet, Riley realizes that he is in the arms of a knight in a suit of armor!

"*Mi dispiace,*" a voice mumbles from behind the facemask of the metal helmet. "I am sorry, I did not see you. This helmet makes it very difficult to see. I surely do not know how they did manage to walk, let alone fight, in this armor in medieval days."

Nearly trembling with fear, Riley and Delaney grab their aunt and wrap themselves in the folds of her skirt. Riley looks up at Sister Philomena, his eyes begging for an explanation of this talking armored knight and court jester, and for reassurance that this place is going to be safe.

"You're okay," assures Sister Philomena. "It's tradition. During the Palio, members of various city neighborhoods dress in costumes of every kind. The neighborhoods are known as *contrade*, and there are seventeen different ones in the area. They've been doing this for the last 500 or so years, so this dates back to the early 1500s. While you're here, you'll see all kinds of people in medieval and Renaissance outfits. The word Renaissance means rebirth. It was a period when people rediscovered things like art and science from ancient times—and by ancient times we mean way before the Roman Empire and the time of Jesus' birth. At the time of the Renaissance, business and art were growing rapidly, and every town or community wanted to be number one. The spirit of competition led these towns and communities to sponsor all kinds of games and festivals. The Palio came out of that competitive spirit.

"The towns and communities of the Renaissance eventually led to the formation of the seventeen *contrade*, the different parishes or neighborhoods that make up the town of Siena," explains Sister Philomena. "People from each *contrada* are very proud of their neighborhood and are very loyal to one another. It's like a brotherhood. In fact, some people are so loyal, they won't even marry someone from another *contrada*. And, they are very competitive.

When we go to the Palio parade and race tomorrow, you'll see that each *contrada* has its own name, its own logo, and its own anthem, flag, costume, and church. It's been the same for centuries."

"Do we belong to a *contrada?*" asks Delaney.

"No, but the Vincenti family belong to the Aquila or eagle contrada, and so we will cheer for them," advises Sister Philomena.

Suddenly, out of nowhere, a ghostly white-haired figure emerges from a dark corner of the entry hall. Riley nearly jumps out of his shoes and grabs his aunt's hand, ready to run as fast as he can back through those big bronze doors to the outside. Delaney gasps, stumbling backwards at the sight and falling on her bottom.

"Wait! It's not a ghost! No such thing as a ghost!" Riley reassures himself. Straining to see through the darkness, he realizes that the ghost-like figure is actually a pale-faced old woman with hair so white it looks like snow.

"*Sorella Philomena*," the old woman says. "*Benvenuti.* Welcome to my home." The woman and Sister Philomena exchange the typical Italian hello, brushing cheeks and air-kissing, and then begin conversing in Italian. When Riley hears his name and Delaney's, he realizes that they are being introduced, and puts out

his hand. The old woman shakes Riley's hand and then pats Delaney on the cheek.

"This is Mrs. Vincenti, children. We shall follow her up the staircase" instructs Sister Philomena. The white-haired lady, now smiling and no longer so spooky looking, leads them up the marble staircase and into a room that they are surprised to see is filled with sunlight. The room smells old, it has a high ceiling, and its walls and entire ceiling are covered with artwork. The room seems almost as big to Riley as his entire house back home. Then he figures that an old palace like this should have big rooms and lots of paintings on the walls, and maybe even a ghost or two.

CHAPTER THREE

PIAZZA DEL CAMPO

Across the room, bright sunlight streams in through huge open doors. Mrs. Vincenti signals to her visitors to go towards the doors and have a look. "From out on that balcony, you children are going to have the best view of the entire Palio race and the famous parade, the *Corteo Storico*, leading up to it!"

"Awesome," gasps Riley as he takes a step outside. He's amazed by what he sees in front of him.

Rising high over the main square, called the *piazza*, is a tall red stone tower topped by a white fortress and gleaming bell tower that seems to pierce the bright blue sky. Riley cups his hands around his eyes because the sun reflecting off of the tower is so bright it hurts his eyes. To the right and beneath the tower he can see a building that looks like an ancient castle or palace. In front of the tower and castle, men are erecting scaffolding and setting up bleachers around the grand *piazza*.

Sister Philomena, watches happily as Riley and Delaney take in the entire scene, which delights her as much as it does them.

"That tower is called the Mangia Tower. It got its name from the Italian word *mangiare*, which as you know means *to eat*. The tower was very expensive to construct, and the local people thought that building it would eat up all the town's money, so they named it *mangia*—in Italian, *it eats*.

"The tower was built in the 1300s and is over 100 meters high—that's more than 300 feet. Imagine how challenging it was to build something so tall way back then. They didn't have cranes or motorized machines in the 1300s; they relied on ropes and pulleys and strong men. But the tower was necessary for their security. The Sienese soldiers would stand watch in

the tower so that they could alert people if they saw invaders coming toward the town. Then the troops would close off the gateways and portals into the city to keep the bad guys out."

The children are fascinated to hear their aunt tell them about the history of this city, and Sister Philomena continues. "To the right of the tower is the Palazzo Pubblico or the Public Palace. It was built many, many, years ago as the city government office. Today it houses a museum as well as city offices.

"See the big circle in the center of its tower with the big letters, IHS. You should recognize that as the symbol for Jesus Christ. Well, it is also the crest chosen by Saint Bernardine, one of the most famous saints from this area. You'll see that symbol in a lot of places in Siena. This is a very Christian and holy place."

Riley studies the huge clamshell-shaped *piazza*, the Piazza del Campo, that occupies the entire area between them and the Mangia Tower. He and Delaney watch as men begin dumping truckloads of reddish-brown dirt inside a ring that goes all the way around the *piazza*. "Why are they doing that?" Riley asks.

"They're putting down dirt and sand for the horse race," answers Sister Philomena. "It is a tradition to have the horses run on local Siena soil, and in addition, it is safer for the horses to run on dirt and sand than on the bricks of the *piazza*. Once the race is run, they'll remove the dirt and sand.

"Here's an interesting fact for you: that reddish dirt the men are putting down is from area farms and it is referred to as the *terra Siena*. In boxes of crayons you will sometimes find a reddish color called *sienna* or *burnt sienna*. That crayon gets its name and the color from this very dirt, the *terra Siena*."

"How do you know so much?" asks Delaney, amazed by her aunt.

"I went to school and I studied hard, just like you will!" smiles Sister Philomena as she gives her niece a hug.

Mrs. Vincenti joins her visitors and explains, "Soon they will be putting up dining tables in the *piazzas* of the various *contrade*. The entire city will eat dinner outside tonight."

"Do we get to eat outside, too?" wonders Delaney.

"You most certainly do!" assures Mrs. Vincenti. "We, along with everyone from our section of the city, will be served a grand out-of-doors feast."

"Look over there, I see men twirling flags!" interrupts Riley.

"Yes, they're practicing. Each of the *contrada* has flag twirlers who will perform tonight, and tomorrow before the Palio. It is all so very exciting!" exclaims Mrs. Vincenti.

Just then all the bells of the city's many churches and the bells in the Mangia Tower begin to toll. The sound is deafening. The crowds cheer and bands begin to play. "Let's hurry and unpack and wash up so we can join in the festivities!" says an excited Sister Philomena.

Riley keeps a very firm grip on his little sister's hand as they enter the street with Sister Philomena and Mrs. Vincenti. The street is a madhouse, but a happy one. People seem to be bursting with joy—young people, old people, everyone mixing in. Many people are dressed in colorful Renaissance clothing, some have their faces painted in the colors of their *contrada*, and everyone has a flag to wave. "Look over there; see the jugglers and acrobats," cries Riley. "This is crazy!"

Delaney stops and stares, thinking she sees the couple who were making a scene at the train station. "Aunt Philomena, those people were at the train station and they were fighting." She tries to shout over the crowd noise while struggling to keep up with her aunt.

"Come, let's hurry," commands Sister Philomena, taking Delaney's hand and pulling her close. It's so busy and noisy that Delaney doesn't have a chance to tell her aunt about the couple.

Bandierine
Del Contrade

Just around the corner from the *palazzo*, they enter into a smaller *piazza* that sits in front of a church. Long dining tables draped with cloths of red and gold, the colors of the Vincenti family's section of the city, and bearing the eagle logo of the Aquila *contrada* fill the small *piazza*. Riley studies the Aquila logo for a while and figures out that it's a double-headed eagle holding a sword in one set of claws, a globe with a cross on top in the other, while a red crown hovers above the eagle's heads. He approves.

Mrs. Vincenti invites her guests to sit with her at the head table. Men dressed in colorful outfits, like the guy who scared them and then took their luggage at the *palazzo*, deliver platters of food. First come platters of sliced bread topped with chopped tomatoes, basil, garlic, and olive oil. Riley knows this is called *bruschetta*, and it's his favorite appetizer. Then antipasto platters with sliced salami, cheese, peppers, hard-boiled eggs, green onions, artichokes, and anchovies are circulated.

"Children, it's best to eat slowly and take small amounts. There is more food coming. More than you can ever eat—and much more than you will ever see in the convent," chuckles Sister Philomena. She is enjoying this outing and the food as much as the children are.

"Where does all the food come from—who makes it all?" questions Delaney.

"The ladies of the previous year's winning *contrada* prepare the meal and the men serve it. It's all part of the tradition."

Sister Philomena ducks as a man carrying two huge platters of spaghetti nearly hits her in the head. The platter in his right hand has regular spaghetti with red tomato sauce, but the platter in his left hand is brimming with *pici Senese*. Pici is a fat spaghetti and here it is served with a special sauce made of olive oil, garlic, a little sage, and crushed pepper—a Siena specialty—spicy but delicious.

Thinking that it's the end of the meal, Riley and Delaney devour their huge plates of pasta—but then come the meat courses, including platters of roasted chicken, sausages, and sliced pork. It all smells so good. This time Riley and Delaney take smaller portions, as their stomachs are getting really full.

Soon after they finish the meat, along come platters of baked fish with roasted vegetables! They've never seen so much food in their entire lives!

Delaney lets out a loud cry, "Ewww!" as she finds herself staring into the face and eyes of a large baked fish. Riley takes a look, laughs, and mostly to tease his sister, helps himself to half the fish.

All during the meal, the band is playing, people are

talking, and the twirlers are hurling giant flags into the air and masterfully catching them just before they hit the ground.

Riley leans back in his chair to take a break from eating. Looking around to see who is seated close to him, he spots the couple from the train. They look like they are arguing again, so he stretches to see if he can hear them.

"Did you hide it good?" he can hear the man ask the woman.

"I did," the woman responds. "I put it there during the last Palio. With all the commotion and celebrating going on, no one paid a bit of attention to me. The sisters were too busy taking care of the tourists to notice me. I just blended in."

"You better be right," the man said in a threatening voice.

Riley's curiosity is tweaked. Hide what? What sisters? He wonders if he should tell his aunt about what he just heard, but decides to let it go.

When they are all finished eating, the people leave the *piazza* to stroll the narrow streets of Siena. The streets are cobblestone and free of cars. Although the main streets have bright streetlights, the side streets look like dark passageways lit by old-fashioned oil-burning lamps. Riley peeks through an alleyway and sees that it opens into another small *piazza*, which like the Aquila *piazza* is lined with dining tables and people feasting. Mrs. Vincenti leads them into a side street, and after walking up a little hill, they find another brightly lit street filled with people walking arm in arm. It seems like everyone is out walking off their dinners and no one wants to go home.

"Are we going to stay up all night?" asks Delaney. "We never get to stay up late in the convent. Besides, everyone else is still up!"

"Yes, people are still out, but they will soon be going home and to bed, as we will. Tomorrow is going to be a very exciting and busy day. I suggest we go back to the Palazzo Vincenti and get some sleep," cautions Sister Philomena.

"Besides, you two have never slept in a palace before. Let's see what that's like."

CHAPTER FOUR

ODD BLESSINGS

The morning sun bursts through the shutters in the room where Riley is sleeping and its brilliant rays seem to bore holes right through his closed eyelids. Shaking the sleep out of his head, Riley quietly gets out of bed and crosses the room. He pushes open the shutters expecting to see a continuation of the excitement from the night before, but below him, in the Piazza del Campo, there is nothing but an eerie quiet. "Did I sleep through the Palio?" he wonders.

Riley wanders around the *palazzo* until he finds Sister Philomena and Delaney, who are already up and dressed.

"Riley, hurry and get ready, we're going to the Jockeys' Mass in the Chapel of the Palazzo Pubblico," says Sister Philomena. "His Eminence, the Archbishop of Siena, is celebrating! It's a special Mass for the horse riders and it starts at 7:45. We want to get there in time to get a good seat."

"Another early morning Mass? You said we were on vacation. Don't you ever take a vacation from going to church?" Riley asks rather grumpily.

"Never, never, never! We never take a vacation from the Lord," laughs Sister Philomena. "You know that. He is always with us and we must be thankful that He has afforded us this wonderful holiday. Besides, the Jockeys' Mass is something special. Trust me, you'll find it interesting."

Riley soon discovered that his aunt was right. The Mass was fantastic. All the jockeys were dressed in the bright colors of their particular *contrada*. There were trumpets and drums and loud singing. The Archbishop preached about good sportsmanship and how the jockeys are not only representatives of their *contrade,* but also goodwill ambassadors for the entire city of Siena. He also talked about Saint Catherine, one of the really famous saints from Siena, and how her family belonged to the *Contrada dell'Oca* (that's the *Contrada* of the Goose). Imagine that, a *contrada* with its very own saint! At the end of Mass, the Archbishop added prayers asking for Saint Catherine to pray to God for His guidance. But he asked her to remain neutral and not just help out the *Oca*, but to pray for a safe and fair race for all.

When Sister Philomena and the children return to their *palazzo*, brunch is being served to a crowd of guests in the big sunny room. A buffet table covered with a colorful array of dishes is set up in the center of the room.

Waiters walk around with trays of drinks: juice, pop, water, milk, wine—just about anything a person would want.

Because they ate until they were about to explode last night, Riley and Delaney aren't hungry just yet. Delaney takes one of the big napkins from the table and drapes it over her head. Pretending to be a princess, she bows to Riley. Riley joins her game and takes her by the hand and leads her around the room. Pretending to be art experts, they study the pictures on the walls, and then they go out onto the balcony to the sounds of cheering voices. Delaney curtsies and Riley bows, pretending the applause is for them.

"We are living in a palace and are being treated like kings and queens," smiles Riley as he and Delaney help themselves to sodas and little sandwiches being offered by the waiter.

Riley and Delaney pull two chairs to the edge of the balcony and imagine they are "royals" observing the crowd and all the activities taking place in front of them. Even though the horse race is still a few hours away, people are jamming the bleachers below and filling up the entire *piazza*. Colorful banners and flags are flying from all the balconies surrounding the Piazza del Campo. Singing rings forth from different groups in every direction.

"There are so many people here," observes Riley. "I sure hope there will be enough room for the horses to run. The track around the *piazza* looks really small now. Do you think the horses will be bothered by all the noise and people?"

"Look down there," says Delaney, pointing to the crowd below their balcony. "It's the man and woman we saw at the train station—remember, the ones who were arguing. She's still picking on him! Look, she keeps giving him a package, then he makes her take it back—back and forth, back and forth it goes. They're funny. Do you suppose she's still calling him an idiot?"

"He looks really annoyed," observes Riley. "Oh, look! He just grabbed the package from her and now he's sitting on it. Now they both look annoyed!"

Riley tells his sister about what he heard while eavesdropping at the meal the night before. They are in the process of deciding if they should tell their aunt when she interrupts them.

"Delaney, Riley, it's nearly three o'clock. We have to make our way to the Aquila *contrada's* parish church for the blessing," urges Sister Philomena.

"But Aunt Philomena, we already went to church. Don't you remember? We want to watch what's happening in the *piazza*," pleads Riley.

"We'll be back in plenty of time to watch the parade and race. Besides, the race cannot begin until the horses are blessed."

35

Horses blessed? What is she talking about?

The *piazza* in front of the little church of the Aquila *contrada* is filled with people. Riley recognizes many of them as guests from the Vincenti party.

"*Sorella Philomena, vieni qui,*" Mrs. Vincenti calls out loudly from the doorway to the church.

Taking Delaney and Riley securely by their hands, Sister Philomena pulls them through the crowd and into the small church where Mrs. Vincenti is waiting for them. They push their way to the front, where they find an empty pew.

"What is going on? I need to see," demands Delaney. Sister Philomena pulls the children in close to her and puts her arms around them protectively.

A bell rings and the crowd in the church grows silent. From behind the altar come six altar servers; the first pair is carrying holy water, the next candles, and the third pair has incense. Two priests dressed in cassocks and albs follow after them. The mood in the church seems quite pious.

Suddenly the sound of hooves *clippity-clopping, clippity-clopping* against the marble floor echoes throughout the small church.

Riley and Delaney sit with mouths wide open as they watch the Aquila jockey ride his horse up the center aisle of the church to the altar and then dismount.

A horse in the church! This is crazy!

The priest first incenses the horse and jockey, says some prayers, and then sprinkles them with holy water.

"*Vai e torna vincitore,*" commands the priest in a loud, booming voice.

Riley and Delaney look at each other quizzically and then look to their aunt for explanation.

"In English it means, '*Go and return a winner.*'"

Immediately, both priests pull Aquila *contrada* scarves from under their albs and begin waving them. The entire church erupts, singing a great *Amen.*

The jockey gets back on the horse, turns, and rides out of the church to go prepare for the race, encouraged by the cheers and applause of the entire congregation.

THE PALIO

"I hear them coming! I hear them coming!" shout Riley and Delaney as they reclaim their chairs on the balcony of the *Palazzo Vincenti.*

The sounds of drums beating and trumpets blaring grow louder as the bands of the *contrade* march from the gateways of Siena toward the Piazza del Campo.

A hush comes over the crowd. People standing on the balconies, sitting in the bleachers, and packed into the *piazza* strain to hear the marchers. Eager faces are everywhere. Pride swells in the hearts of the Sienese people. This is their special day!

The next several hours are filled with pageantry as the parade pours through the portals of the Piazza del Campo. The participants include groups from nearby towns, each with their own decorated cart or float; Sienese business and trades people on foot; and mounted *carabinieri* officers. Next come the pages, drummers, and trumpeters of the seventeen *contrade,* all dressed in their colorful Renaissance costumes.

Riley picks out the two men they encountered in the *palazzo* last evening, the one in the striped red and gold outfit and the other in the suit of armor. Funny how last night they were scary, but today, they fit right in!

"There's Mrs. Vincenti!" Riley shouts to his aunt just as the white-haired lady passes under their balcony. She is dressed in a beautiful red and gold gown and riding in an elegant horse-drawn carriage. She waves to them and blows kisses. Delaney laughs in pure delight and waves back.

"Oh, yes! She's among the group of people that represent the city authorities and noble families of Siena," says an elderly gentleman standing behind them.

"Oh," says Riley, who has just figured out that a woman who lives in a palace certainly must be of nobility. His aunt certainly takes them to some pretty cool places!

By now the crowd seems almost out of control. Thousands of people in the *piazza* are waving colorful hats and scarves. Spontaneously, groups of spectators burst into songs. Cheers and jeers fill the air each time a new group of *contrade* pages marches through the portals. Flag twirlers stop in front of the Palazzo Pubblico and toss their flags higher and higher into the air.

"An ox-drawn cart!" shouts Delaney. "Look! Four white oxen!"

The crowd erupts into an unbelievable roar as the final cart enters the *piazza*. "That's the Palio," said the older gentleman, pointing to the huge flag held high over the cart. "The Palio is actually a banner that will be awarded to the *contrada* that wins the race."

"*Kahboom!!!*"

The reverberation of a thundering blast sets Riley and Delaney back on their heels. Riley grabs hold of Delaney, thinking something awful has happened.

"Don't worry," the older gentleman shouts over the noise. "That's the cannon blast that signals that the horses and jockeys are approaching."

The crowd reaches a level of utter pandemonium as the racehorses and jockeys enter the *piazza*.

"It's time, children, it's time!" Sister Philomena seems almost giddy as she embraces Riley and Delaney. Riley has never seen her enjoy something this much. What would the Pope think if he could see her now?

"Look over there," the elderly gentleman directs their attention to the horses lining up along a rope stretched across the track. "The jockeys draw numbers, then ride the horses around the track in the order they've been given. Do you see the men drawing a second rope across the track? The horses have to remain between those two ropes until the race begins."

Riley, Delaney, and Sister Philomena watch intently as the horses approach the ropes. Nine of the horses are now between the lines.

"The jockeys bump and push each other trying to get on the inside, which is supposed to be the best starting point," explains the man. "After nine horses are in line between the two ropes, the #10 horse runs up and crosses the line. That starts the race!"

The crowd grows quiet as it waits and watches.

The #10 horse nears the line. Tension mounts. The crowd erupts just as the #10 horse reaches the rope! But the jockey pulls back on the reins and the horse backs up and turns away.

A collective "Oh!" passes through the *piazza*.

"False start," says the gentleman. "The tenth jockey somehow didn't go straight—perhaps he's teasing them. Often there are false starts. But once the race starts, watch very carefully—the entire race is over in less than two minutes."

"And there they go!" shouts the elderly gentleman. Everyone crushes against the edge of the balcony to get a better look.

The horses and jockeys scramble around the lopsided *piazza*. The turns in the racecourse are so tight that the horses and their riders bunch up in the corners. Two jockeys fall off, or are really pushed off, their horses.

"It's okay," shouts the old man. "It's the horse that has to finish the race, not the jockey!"

Around they go again. Crashing. Dashing. Stumbling. Pushing. Shoving. The two horses without jockeys continue to run the race. Suddenly another jockey tumbles to the ground. His horse keeps running—it has nowhere else to go.

The crowd is out of control as the horses begin the last lap. Screaming. Shouting. Crying. Arms flailing. Then, as the winning horse with jockey still on crosses the finish line, the people let out a roar the likes of which Riley has never heard before.

"We won! We won!" The people on their balcony and an entire section of people in the *piazza* below their *palazzo* burst out in song—it's the Aquila *contrada* anthem.

Riley, Delaney, and Sister Philomena look at each other in a state of confusion. Then it dawns on them that their *contrada's* horse, the Aquila's horse, just won the race.

"Hurry, we must run down to the giant cathedral, the Duomo," the gentleman commands with tears in his eyes. "This is the happiest day of my life! It's been ten years… I can't believe it. Here, I'll carry the girl. Sister, you take the boy by the hand and follow close behind me."

Hundreds of people pour into the street waving

Aquila flags and singing its anthem. Sister Philomena, Riley, Delaney, and the gentleman are engulfed in the crowd and then pushed down the street in a giant wave of humanity.

The rush of the crowd carries them straight into the Duomo, the huge Cathedral of Santa Maria at the edge of town. As they get close to the Duomo, the crowd becomes quiet. Suddenly everyone begins singing a sacred song, the *Te Deum*.

"This is really wild. Nobody, absolutely nobody, back home would believe this! Look there, it's the Aquila horse and jockey—inside the cathedral! I don't understand. Why are everyone, and the horse, inside the cathedral?" Riley asks.

"To honor the Blessed Mother, the Virgin of the Vow. She is the patron saint of this Palio," says the gentleman, who is now holding Delaney up high above the crowd so she can see. "And to give thanks for a safe race and thanks for having the opportunity to win."

"This is crazy!" exclaims Riley, again.

"I know," laughs Sister Philomena. "Isn't it great! It's so sacred and yet almost sacrilegious!"

The celebrations continue throughout the evening. Back at the *piazza* of the Aquila *contrada* tables are again set for another grand feast. Sister Philomena,

Riley, and Delaney now definitely claim Aquila as their *contrada* and the people of Siena have unofficially adopted them.

There is food and merrymaking in the *piazza* until the wee hours of the morning.

It is closer to dawn than dusk by the time Sister Philomena walks the children back to the *palazzo*. "I am going to let the two of you sleep in tomorrow morning. In fact, after all this excitement, I may also sleep in for a change!

"We will find a Mass late in the day, perhaps near the Santuario de Santa Caterina. Visiting the home of Saint Catherine of Siena would be a nice thing for us to do."

CHAPTER SIX

THE DAY AFTER

Bong… *bong… bong… bong… bong….* Riley squeezes his eyes closed as he counts the number of clangs of the bell from the Mangia Tower. *Bong… bong… bong… bong… bong… bong.* "…Nine, ten, eleven," then quiet. "Oh my gosh, it must be eleven o'clock in the morning!" Riley jumps out of bed and runs to find his sister. Together they rush to the balcony of the party room to see if the Palio is still in progress. Disappointment fills their hearts when they see that the Piazza del Campo has been put back almost to normal. Men are scooping the red earth back into trucks. The bleachers are being dismantled, and bags filled with trash are being thrown into garbage trucks. Today, the *piazza* looks sad and lonely.

"It seems like a dream. It was so much fun and now it's over," sighs Delaney.

"I know. Maybe we can come back some time— maybe even with Mom and Dad," suggests Riley. "But I doubt that we will ever get to stay in a palace like this one again."

Just then their aunt comes into the room. "I have some fruit and cheese, and bowls of cereal, too. I also have a plan for today's activities."

"Let me see. I bet it involves going to a church," laughs Riley.

"*Esatto*!" exclaims Sister Philomena. "How right you are! But we are also going to explore the life of the famous Saint Catherine of Siena. I predict that you will just love her. We'll begin by visiting the Basilica Cateriniana di San Domenico and then we'll go see the house where Saint Catherine was born and lived as a little girl. Saint Catherine of Siena is the patron saint of Italy and of all Europe. It would be a shame to be in Siena and not visit these two holy places at least."

"What did she do to become so famous?" questions Riley.

"She is best known for her letters," states Sister Philomena. "Although she didn't learn to read and write until near the time of her death, she dictated hundreds of letters to help people know and love God. And, she became a friend of the Pope."

"Like you're a friend of the Pope?" asks Delaney as she plays with the cheese and fruit on her plate.

"Not exactly," responds Sister Philomena. "I work for the Pope, which is a great honor. Saint Catherine, however, 'advised' the Pope and gave him confidence. I would never dream of telling the Pope what to do, as

she did. Now children, eat up! We need to go exploring."

"Holy cow, this place is huge—and empty!" cries Delaney, as they enter the Gothic style church, the Basilica Cateriniana di San Domenico. "It's not like the churches in Rome."

Sister Philomena is amused that Delaney notices the difference. "This church is built according to the Dominican Rule—nothing is supposed to separate those attending Mass from the presider, who is the preacher, the priest. That's why there aren't any columns or side aisles—nothing to block the parishioners' view of the priest at the altar."

As they approach the main altar, Sister Philomena points out the burial crypts of the members of Saint Catherine's family that are behind the altar. Delaney continues to be grossed out by the thought of all the dead bodies buried in the churches of Italy.

"Look into that reliquary," directs Sister Philomena as they approach a smaller altar on the right. "Tell me what you see."

"I see a glass jar. There is a gold crown inside and lots of jewels on the outside," says Delaney. "It's beautiful!"

"Yeah. Look, that looks like a crown of thorns on top," says Riley. "What does it mean?"

"Good observations. The story goes that when Catherine was young, people often made fun of her because of her piety and goodness. Their teasing hurt her feelings, but she put up with it because of her deep love of Jesus Christ. Once, Saint Catherine had a vision of Jesus in which He offered her a choice between the crown of thorns and a gold crown studded with jewels. She chose the crown of thorns so she would be more like Him. You see, Jesus also was taunted and ridiculed on earth, and then given a crown of thorns in dishonor. Catherine somehow understood that by lovingly accepting her plight here on earth that the crown of gold and jewels would be hers in heaven," explains Sister Philomena.

"What's in here?" asks curious Delaney, as they approach a brightly lit alcove with paintings on the walls.

"It's the Chapel of Saint Catherine," explains Sister Philomena.

"What's that in the middle, behind the bars?" probes Delaney, straining to see the object on the altar at the rear of the chapel.

"Oh, oh!" says Riley. "I bet I know what it is. Aunt Philomena, is that another skull?"

"Oh, yuck!" exclaims Delaney.

"Shush," whispers Sister Philomena with a chuckle. She understands how these things might gross out

Delaney, but she also knows that both she and Riley are fascinated by death and ancient burial practices. Aren't we all, she thinks to herself.

"Yes, it's a skull. It's the head of Saint Catherine."

The children gasp and start to pull away.

"Don't be silly. It cannot hurt you. Besides, Catherine was one person who never feared death. She taught that life on earth is just a temporary state and that we really belong in our eternal home, that's in heaven with Jesus."

"Look at those pictures on the walls!" exclaims a distracted Delaney, taking notice of the beautiful murals covering the walls of the chapel. "Is that Saint Catherine holding a man's head? Gross!"

"It is indeed," says Sister Philomena. "That picture shows you just how unafraid Catherine was of death.

"The young man in the picture, the one whose head is chopped off, was named Niccolo di Tuldo. The story goes that he had plotted to overthrow the government officials of Siena. Not a good idea. Niccolo was caught, tried by those he tried to overthrow, and condemned to death. A priest went to visit him in the jail, but Niccolo would have nothing to do with the priest. Niccolo had become extremely violent and angry—no doubt he was possessed by the devil. As a last hope, the priest asked for Catherine to visit Niccolo. It worked! She was such a pure and holy person that just her presence helped Niccolo to calm down and

confront his past. That night, after Catherine left him, Niccolo asked for the priest to come back. He was able to go to confession and received Holy Communion.

"By the day of his execution, Niccolo had become very calm and even welcomed death, knowing that he would soon be with God. But he also wanted Catherine to be with him. By the time Catherine arrived, his neck was already positioned on the executioner's block. Catherine kissed Niccolo and then made the sign of the cross on his neck. The man was put to death with a smile on his face, repeating the names of Jesus and Catherine. As his head landed in her lap, Catherine claimed she saw Niccolo's soul fly heavenward. See, in the picture, the angels are carrying his soul to heaven. Catherine later remarked that she was sorry that she could not accompany Niccolo to heaven that day."

"Saint Catherine was some gutsy lady," observes Riley. "What else did she do?"

"Well, it may seem odd to you now, but her life was really filled with beauty. Next we'll go down to the Santuario di Santa Caterina—it's the house where she grew up. There are lots of pictures on the walls of the house which tell the story of Catherine's youth and holiness."

CHAPTER SEVEN

SAINT CATHERINE'S CELL

"**A**wesome!" cries Delaney, as she spins around to get a good look at four walls that are just covered with nearly life-size drawings. The children and their aunt are now in the *camerata* or dormitory where Saint Catherine and her brothers and sisters slept as children.

"Let me tell you her story," says Sister Philomena. "Catherine was born on March 25th, 1347, and was the twenty-third child born into her family. She actually had a twin sister who died as a baby, just after the girls were baptized.

"As a child, Catherine was a peculiarly happy and charming girl. She was only six years old when she discovered that she was blessed with a strong calling. One day, as she was walking home from school with her brother Stefano, Catherine stopped to admire the church of Saint Dominic, the one we just visited. As she looked toward the church, Catherine had a vision of Jesus Christ seated on a splendid throne, dressed and crowned as a pope, and flanked by the Apostles

Peter, Paul, and John. She froze and did not move for a long time as Jesus raised his hand and blessed her. This vision filled her with joy. Stefano saw that she wasn't moving and feared something bad had happened to her—so he shouted at her. That broke her trance. Catherine cried and cried because her beatific vision had vanished.

"Catherine's mother wanted her to marry, so she began looking for a husband for Catherine when the girl was only twelve. Catherine would have nothing to do with it, as she had already pledged herself to Jesus. Her brothers and sisters were confused by her commitment, and they teased and tormented her, as did other children and even adults. She was punished and forced to do menial tasks, but it didn't make any difference. No matter what they did or said to her, Catherine remained a happy and devout girl.

"That picture over there shows Catherine cutting her beautiful blond hair. She did that to try and make herself less attractive to young men.

"As a kind of punishment, and to try to persuade Catherine to consider leading a so-called 'normal' life, Catherine's mother made her share a room with her brother. But this, too, had no effect on Catherine. She became even more determined to pursue a righteous life style.

"One day, Catherine's father found her in her room, the very room that we're in, and she was on her knees

praying. As he peered through the door he saw a snow-white dove nestled upon Catherine's head. See, just like that picture shows," she said, pointing to one of the paintings on the wall. "He called for her mother, but by the time she arrived, the dove had vanished. From that day on, Catherine's parents began to understand that their daughter was destined for higher things.

"Finally, Catherine was allowed to join a Dominican Order as a nun and dress in their traditional habit. There were no convents in the area, so she began to live under religious rule in her own home. She stayed in a tiny room of her parents' house, this very house where we are standing, and lived as a religious recluse for several years. The only person she would speak to was her spiritual confessor, and the only thing she ate was bread, a few herbs, and water. During those years she spent almost all her waking time in prayer."

"Come over here and see this, children. This is the tiny cell where Catherine lived and prayed all the time."

Riley and Delaney look through an iron gate at the back of the *camerata* and into a tiny brick-enclosed room. As they lean against the gate, it moves! Riley gives it a little shove, and the gate swings open on squeaky hinges.

"Oops!"

Sister Philomena, Riley, and Delaney can't resist. They quietly slip into the tiny cell. It's only about three feet wide by nine feet long.

"You mean she actually lived in here?" Delaney cannot imagine anyone living in such a little space and just praying all the time.

"It is pretty hard to imagine, isn't it?

"Riley, keep your fingers off the walls, please. Dear Saint Catherine, pray for us!" Sister Philomena is a little nervous about allowing the children into this sacred place, and says a prayer of intercession.

"But the bricks feel so cool, smooth, and soft," comments Riley as he continues to touch the wall. "Hey, look, here's a loose brick." Before Sister can stop him, Riley removes the brick so he can feel it and to see if he can figure out why it's loose.

"There's a plastic bag stuck back behind there," says a startled Riley. "It looks like there's something inside it. That's strange—I don't think plastic bags had been invented yet in Saint Catherine's time."

"How curious," says Sister Philomena, pulling the plastic bag from its hiding place. "It looks as if it was placed here recently. Do you suppose someone was using this cell as a hiding place?"

Suddenly they hear loud footsteps coming from the stairs that lead to the *camerata*. They look at each other

in panic. A feeling comes over them—it's that feeling you get when you are caught doing something you are definitely not supposed to be doing.

"Let's get out of here," whispers Sister Philomena. Her investigator instinct takes over as she slips the plastic bag into the pocket of her habit and pushes the brick back into the wall. As they step out of the cell and pull the gate closed, a large figure wearing the Dominican nun's habit appears before them.

"*Buona sera*," says a deep, husky voice. How strange! It sounds like a man's voice, but the person is dressed in a nun's habit.

Delaney stares at the nun's face. She finds the face quite odd and out of place, but a little familiar.

"*Buona sera*," responds Sister Philomena. "We are just admiring the paintings in this room. Come children, it's time to go."

Sister Philomena pulls Riley and Delaney through the doorway past the nun. They rush up the stone steps to the entry of the Sanctuary, find the exit, and escape into the streets of Siena.

"Let's hurry," she urges, as they enter a narrow street leading away from the Sanctuary. "Let's go back to the palace and look in this plastic bag."

"You took it?" Riley says in disbelief.

"Yes."

"Isn't that stealing?" asks Delaney.

"Let's assume I'm working on another investigation—now shush and run!" demands Sister Philomena.

As they turn into a dark side street, they hear footsteps running after them. The husky voice of the nun shouts out something in Italian. Sister Philomena's radar for danger is activated.

"Run, run!" commands Sister Philomena. They turn into another dark street. "This way. We're being followed. We have to ditch whoever it is!"

Riley grabs Delaney and drags her as fast as her little legs will carry her. Back through the narrow streets they run, in and out of dark corridors and back alleyways. "It's a dead end!" shouts Riley as they round yet another corner.

"No it's not. It only looks that way," pants Sister Philomena. Just as they reach what at first looks like a blank wall, they notice a small opening in the corner. Slipping through the slot, they find themselves facing the *Palazzo Vincenti*.

They quickly enter the palace, out of breath but finally feeling safe. Sister guides the children quickly to the third floor where they enter a small private chapel. Truly safe at last, Sister Philomena sits and says a quiet prayer. Then she puts her hand inside the pocket of her habit and pulls out the plastic bag.

"What is this?" she says, examining the clear plastic bag and its contents. "Do you suppose that nun was coming to retrieve it?" She feels guilty for having taken the bag from the site of Saint Catherine's home, but something is not right. Her intuition tells her that the bag is suspicious, and that she needs to examine it. It might be of value to the Church. If not, she can always return it to its hiding place.

Inside the bag are two documents. One of the documents is a piece of ordinary white paper with some writing on it. The writing could have come from a typewriter, but more likely printed off a computer. The other one looks as if it might crumble at the touch of a finger. It's yellowish and the handwriting looks really fancy and old fashioned. It has to be centuries old.

A MYSTERY UNFOLDS

"This is a ransom note!" exclaims Sister Philomena as she examines one of the documents from the plastic bag. "And it is addressed to the Holy Father. I just knew I should have taken this bag and its contents—I just knew it!"

Looking at the other document, the old-looking one, Sister Philomena frowns.

"Can I see?" asks Riley.

"Me too?" says Delaney, pulling at her aunt's sleeve.

"We must be careful. This old document seems very fragile. Like the ransom note, it is also appears to be in Italian but this one is handwritten," observes Sister Philomena.

"Read the ransom note to us!" Riley is all excited. He senses yet another adventure brewing.

"Oh my heavens! Oh my heavens!" Sister Philomena is stunned.

"The ransom note claims that the old document is

one of Saint Catherine's letters to Pope Gregory XI. It says that what I have here in my hand is one-half of the letter. The other half is still being kept in France, in Avignon, at the Palace of the Popes. The Holy Father and the Vatican can have both halves of the letter only if and when the Holy Father pays the ransom. This is strange. The note does not include a ransom amount; there's a blank space. Perhaps the crooks haven't yet decided on the ransom, and that's why the letter was hidden.

"These documents, if they really are letters from Saint Catherine to Pope Gregory XI, are priceless."

Sister Philomena frowns as she carefully opens and reads from the older paper. "Good heavens! I am sure this letter has something to do with Pope Gregory XI moving the papal offices from Avignon back to Rome. But it reads like it's written in half sentences." Then she realizes what has happened. "Oh dear Lord, this priceless letter has actually been cut in two!"

"I thought the popes always lived in Rome or at the Vatican," says Riley.

"Not always," explains Sister Philomena. "A long time ago, in the 1300s, the Papacy, the Pope and his office, the Holy See, was moved out of Italy to a town named Avignon, in a part of the country that is now in France. It was a time of uncertainty, and so the Pope was safer in Avignon. This letter, if it's real, and in one piece, would provide a very important link between Saint Catherine and Pope Gregory XI and his move back to Rome."

"What are we going to do?" asks Riley. "That nun or person who found us in the sanctuary is probably the one that hid the bag and knows we have it."

"I think it was a fake nun," adds Delaney. "The voice was too rough for a nun, and she had whiskers on her face like Daddy gets sometimes. I'm scared."

"Fake nun? That's a new one for me," muses Sister Philomena. She looks at Riley.

"I don't think it was a real nun either. Too mean-sounding. The voice seemed familiar to me but I don't know from where; it was definitely a weird voice; more like a man's voice," says Riley. "If the person was there to retrieve the bag and couldn't, she—or maybe he—may become desperate. Do you think they will try to destroy the other half of the letter—wouldn't that be bad?"

"Yes, that is a possibility, and that would be very bad," says Sister Philomena. "However, based on this ransom note, we have every reason to believe that the other half of the letter is still in Avignon. We must try and retrieve it before that nun-person or her people can get to it!

"I must contact the Holy Father and maybe even

Capitano Leo of the Swiss Guard at once. I need the
Holy Father's permission to act on this."

Sister Philomena paces back and forth inside the safety
of the chapel. Riley can tell by the way she is walking
and acting now that she's focusing hard on this case—
it's the way she walks and acts when she is working
on an investigation for the Pope.

Pulling her cell phone from the pocket of her habit,
Sister Philomena punches in the private number for
the Vatican and the Pope. Riley and Delaney try hard
to listen to the conversation, but cannot understand
what she is saying because she is speaking very fast
and in Italian. They watch as she nods and waves her
free hand, shrugs her shoulders a few times, then
shakes her head up and down. Sister Philomena has
been on the phone with the Vatican for nearly a half-
hour now. It appears they are getting a plan together.

"Children, quickly, let's get our things together and
say goodbye to Mrs. Vincenti," urges Sister Philomena
as she closes her cell phone. "Act normally. We can't
let anyone know that we found these documents and
that we know about this ransom situation. I am sure
the Vincentis are not involved, but I have learned from
experience that when you are in the middle of an
investigation such as this one, you should not tell any-

one what you are doing until all the facts are uncovered.

"Hopefully we can get to Avignon yet this evening. We must try to find the other half of the letter before this person can get to it and destroy it. The problem is, we do not know exactly where to look. The ransom note indicates it is being kept in the Palace of the Popes in Avignon. It's a big place!"

"Where exactly is Avignon?" asks Riley.

"It's in the southern part of France, in a region called Provence," says Sister Philomena.

"France! We are in Italy! Where is France and how will we get there?" asks Delaney.

"I am leaving the travel arrangements up to Capitano Leo. He will figure out how we are to get there and where we are to stay, and then he will be accompanying us to Avignon."

Sister Philomena says her goodbyes to Mrs. Vincenti, who offers to have a driver take them to the train station. Sister Philomena insists on taking a taxi, without telling Mrs. Vincenti that she and the children are not going to the train station. As soon as they are in the taxi, Sister Philomena instructs the driver to take them to the address given to her by Capitano Leo. It happens to be the address of an *agriturismo* located just on the outskirts of Siena. An *agriturismo* is a kind of

villa for tourists that is situated on a farm and where people stay and live like locals during their vacation in Italy. Her message from Capitano Leo was to go to this particular location and wait for him. He gave no further explanation.

The taxi driver takes Sister Philomena, Riley, and Delaney to the *agriturismo* which appears to be abandoned. "*Sicura, Sorella?*" he asks in Italian. "*Andate qui?*" Meaning, "Are you sure, Sister, that this is where you want me to leave you?" The place looks empty and deserted, and the taxi driver is concerned about their safety.

"*Si, signore. Grazie.* You may leave us here—we are waiting for a friend."

He shrugs his shoulders, takes his money, and drives away.

Sister Philomena, Riley, and Delaney stand in on edge of a flat lawn that is surrounded by old crumbling buildings and bright yellow sunflowers. Sister Philomena is praying that she understood Capitano Leo correctly and that this is the place they were supposed to meet him. Otherwise, they may be stuck in the middle of nowhere.

CHAPTER NINE

VIA AVIGNON

Chop-chop-chop-chop. The children hear a thumping, thundering noise from off in the distance. It gets louder and louder, closer and closer. Riley searches the sky looking for the source of the noise. Closer and louder it grows.

"Look, there's a helicopter!" exclaims Riley.

"Why, children, I do believe that is Capitano Leo coming for us," says an excited Sister Philomena. "Now it makes sense why he had us come to this location away from town. He needs a flat field on which to land the helicopter."

The *whoosh* of air from the rotating blades of the helicopter crashes and bends the sunflowers away from the landing spot, creating a huge circle around it. Sister Philomena's habit swirls in the wind. Delaney puts her hands over her ears to shut out the noise of the battering blades. Riley shields his eyes from the gusts of dirt blowing all around them.

As Capitano Leo shuts down the engines of the
helicopter, the propeller blades slowly come to a stop.
Now the yellow Vatican insignia is clearly visible on
the side of the helicopter; it's the Pope's miter, crossed
keys, and papal seal.

"It's Vatican One!" shouts Sister Philomena.
"Capitano Leo must be going to fly us to Avignon in
the Pope's helicopter. Surely it is the fastest way to
Avignon. A car, train, and even a commercial plane
would take hours to get us there. How clever!"

The door to the helicopter swings open and out
lopes a big dog. The dog is brownish gray and very
muscular, and looks almost as big as a horse.
Immediately the dog runs to Sister Philomena and
dances all around her.

"What's his name!?" begs Delaney as she tries to
catch the dog. "Did he fly the helicopter?"

Capitano Leo emerges from the door of the helicopter, dressed not in his striped Swiss Guard uniform,
but in a navy blue captain's suit. The breast pocket of
the jacket shows the Vatican symbol and on his shoul-
der are his captain's stripes.

"*Buona sera.*" He greets Sister Philomena and the
children with a bid, *good afternoon.* "You have already
met my trusted flying companion, Bosco, named after
Saint John Bosco. He is my dog and I often like to take

him on rides in the helicopter. The Holy Father doesn't mind. Besides, I thought he might be helpful in our search of the Palace of the Popes.

Riley and Delaney immediately try to make friends with Bosco. The dog, discovering that he has some youthful playmates, dances around the children.

"Good dog, Bosco," says Capitano Leo. "Say hello to *signorina* Delaney." On command, Bosco goes to Delaney, sniffs around her, and then sits in front of her and offers his paw to "shake".

Delaney takes the dog's paw and says, "Pleased to meet you, Bosco."

"Bosco, say hello to Riley," commands Capitano Leo. The dog repeats the same routine, sniffing around Riley. "Now the dog knows your scent and he will be able to find you if you get lost. He is an incredibly smart dog."

"Really?" questions Riley.

"Really," says Capitano Leo. "You go hide behind that tree over there, and Delaney, you go hide in the sunflowers on the other side of the helicopter. We will test Bosco's nose."

On the command, "Bosco, find Riley," the dog turns, sniffs the ground, and follows the scent directly to Riley. "Good dog, Bosco."

Capitano Leo repeats the same drill for the dog to

find Delaney. The dog sniffs the ground and then goes directly to Delaney's hiding spot.

"That's the coolest dog I've ever met," says Riley. He and Delaney hug and pet Bosco.

"Come, let's not waste anymore of the daylight," encourages Capitano Leo. "If we leave now, we should make it to Avignon before dark. It will be a nice flight, and fast.

"Riley, you sit up in front beside me. Delaney and Sister Philomena will sit behind us. Bosco will probably settle down here in between the seats. Put on these earphones so we can hear each other during the flight. You will find that the earphones filter out the noise from the engine and rotors."

The flight from Siena to Avignon is a thrill a minute. As they fly west from Siena toward the coast of Italy, Capitano Leo points out the town of Pisa and the famous landmark, the Leaning Tower of Pisa.

"Look, there it is!" says Riley. "I can actually see the Leaning Tower lean, even from this high up!"

After several more minutes of flying, Capitano Leo points out the coastline of the Italian Riviera and the Mediterranean Sea. Riley recalls his dad showing them the Mediterranean coastline from the window of the big jet when they first flew to Italy. Now the helicopter is flying much lower in the sky and Riley and Delaney are able to make out the villages along the coastline.

"That is the famous Cinque Terre," says Capitano Leo. "It is a famous tourist destination. That area is very beautiful and looks much the same as it did hundreds of years ago. The people who live there are primarily fishermen.

"As for the rest of our flight plan, we will follow the northern Italian Riviera coastline to the border of Italy, then pass over the state of Monaco and its capital city of Monte Carlo, and then onto the French Riviera beginning at Nice, France. You should know that both Monte Carlo and Nice are favorite places for rich and famous people to visit. You will be able to see lots of yachts in the harbors, and beaches dotted with blue umbrellas for the sunbathers.

"After Nice, we will turn inland and fly over the fields, hills, and valleys of Provence until we arrive at our destination, Avignon, France."

Riley wonders how many times before this trip his aunt has gotten to ride in the Pope's helicopter. He is so impressed. He wants to tell the whole world who she is and what she does, but he knows he cannot—it would blow her cover!

"Everyone, look over there—we are coming upon Avignon," says Capitano Leo, pointing his finger out over the nose of the helicopter.

"That's the Rhone River. It runs alongside and through Avignon. We will be landing in that big open field to the right of the river and will have to cross the river by boat. I have radioed ahead for someone to meet us and take us to the other side of the river. From there we will walk, maybe even run, to the Palace of the Popes."

"Is that the Palace of the Popes?" asks Riley, pointing to a massive structure that seems to take up the entire side of town nearest the river. "It makes the Vincenti palace look like a cottage!"

"That's it," says Capitano Leo. "It is the biggest palace in all of Europe. It was built by the Church in the early 1300s.

"You see, at that time things were happening in Rome that made it unsafe for the Pope to stay in Italy. Avignon wasn't yet a part of France and was seen as a neutral country. The decision was made to move the papal residence and offices to Avignon. However, the early popes in Avignon, particularly Clement V and John XXII, kind of lost sight of their mission. They got carried away collecting and hoarding tons of money and precious jewels and building lavish living quarters. The French cardinals who wanted to be close to the Pope liked the fancy living, too."

"In 1370 Gregory XI was elected Pope in Avignon, and saw the need to change things. He and Saint Catherine were good friends and she always encouraged him to do the right thing. Pope Gregory brought the Papacy back to Rome in 1377. After that, this building went through a lot of changes. For a while, a few renegade or false popes tried to keep the palace intact, but they failed. Later different political and religious wars were fought over this property. At one time during the 16th century, this palace was even used as a prison. Little by little, bit by bit, all the treasures—the gold, the paintings, jewels—were destroyed, stolen, or moved to museums. Today the Palace of the Popes is owned by the city of Avignon and is part of France.

They city maintains the palace, but it would be far too costly to restore all the old treasures."

"Hey, that bridge is broken off in the water!" observes Delaney. "Was it bombed?"

"That, my dear, is the famous Pont Saint Benezet, or Saint Benezet Bridge," explains Sister Philomena. "It's been damaged for a very long time. It was built in the 1100s—can you believe it—that's almost a thousand

years ago! At one time it connected Avignon with the other side of the river and was used by by people going to and from wars during the time of the Crusades. Over the years it was destroyed and then rebuilt several times. Finally, as other more substantial bridges were erected, the city decided to leave it broken.

"The bridge is named for Saint Benezet. Legend has it that Benezet was a small shepherd boy who received a message from God to build a bridge in that spot. The townspeople thought he was crazy and was just making up the story. To prove them wrong, Benezet lifted a huge boulder, a boulder so heavy that he should not have been able to lift it, and tossed it into the river. Some say you can still see the boulder in the river, beneath the bridge. Needless to say, the townspeople finally believed Benezet and came together to build the bridge over the river."

As soon as the helicopter is on the ground and the blades have stopped moving, Capitano Leo rushes Sister Philomena, Riley, Delaney, and Bosco, the dog, to a waiting motorboat. Without a word, the driver of the boat whisks them across the river and deposits them at a landing dock on the other side.

"*Merci. Merci beaucoup. Thank you. Thank you very*

much." Capitano Leo says to the motorboat driver.

"*De rein. It was nothing. Dieu soit avec vous. God be with you,*" responds the driver. Then the motorboat speeds away.

Riley turns to Sister Philomena with a look on his face that asks, "That doesn't sound like Italian—what language is it?"

"It's French," explains Sister Philomena. "We are in France now and must try to speak French. But let's hope we're not here long enough to have to talk to very many people."

CHAPTER TEN

THE PALACE OF THE POPES

The four people plus a dog cross the road and enter the city of Avignon through an arched gate in a tall brick wall. Like the wall around the city of Siena, this wall was built centuries ago to protect Avignon from outside invaders.

It is near dusk by the time Capitano Leo leads Sister Philomena, Riley and Delaney through a side door and into a courtyard of the Popes' Palace. Delaney wants to stop and admire the gold lady on top of the church next to the palace, but there is no time.

"That's the Cathedral of Our Lady of the Dome," Sister Philomena explains quickly. "That's a statue of the Virgin Mary on top. This is the church that was used by the popes when they lived in Avignon. Maybe we can visit it later—after we retrieve the ancient letter of Saint Catherine."

"Holy cow, this place is really old—and really big!" comments Riley as they enter into the Palace of the Popes. "Where do we start looking for a little piece of paper in such a gigantic place?"

"We will have to be very organized," responds Sister Philomena. "I will take Delaney and search the Palais Neuf, or new section. Capitano Leo and Riley, why don't you search the Palais Vieux or old areas? The light is fading, so we must work fast. Let's plan on meeting back here in one hour, regardless of what we find."

"How do I know what to look for?" asks Riley.

"We should look for anything that has been recently disturbed—something out of the ordinary," says Sister Philomena.

"How do we know what is ordinary and what is out of the ordinary in a place like this?" questions Riley. He has an overwhelming sense of doom and gloom. He's worried about getting lost, and even more afraid of Delaney getting lost. His sister tends to wander off sometimes, and he's not sure Sister Philomena can handle her all by herself.

Riley follows Capitano Leo and Bosco as they descend into a lower part of the Palais Vieux. The rooms are dark, damp, and foreboding. The Capitano uses his flashlight to probe into the dark nooks and crannies in search of the ancient document. Riley wonders if this is like "looking for a needle in a haystack." Besides, the note they found in Siena didn't clearly say that the other half of Saint Catherine's letter might be here in

the Popes' Palace—they are guessing to some extent. What if they are wrong?

"This doesn't look like much of a palace to me," Delaney complains. Sister Philomena and Delaney are now on the opposite side of the palace from Riley and Capitano Leo. "I thought palaces had lots of big old furniture, silver and gold, and pictures and things."

"Believe me, this palace did have all of those things at one time," says Sister Philomena. "Several of the popes who were here in the 1300s really liked fancy things and they spent lots of the Church's money in this place. They had lavish furnishings, paintings, the 'whole nine yards.' But it's all gone now."

"How come there are holes in the floor in that room?" Delaney asks, changing the subject (which she is very good at).

"Good observation," says Sister Philomena. "That room was once the treasury room. Those early popes had vaults built into the floor so that they could hide jewels, precious metals, and great sums of money. This is a great place for us to look closely for the letter of Saint Catherine. Here, take this flashlight and look inside those two vaults. Holler if you find anything. I will search the other side of the room. When we are finished in here, presuming we don't find anything, we will go look in the old Pope's chambers, otherwise known as his bedroom suite."

"Nothing here," Sister Philomena mutters to herself. An hour has already gone by and it is time to meet Capitano Leo and Riley back near the courtyard. She's hoping that they have had more success in their search than she and Delaney have had.

"Delaney, come, let's go find the men," Sister Philomena calls out.

When there is no answer, Sister Philomena panics. "Where are you, Delaney? Let's go."

Still there is no answer.

Frantically, Sister Philomena begins to retrace her steps, calling out Delaney's name. The palace is now almost completely dark inside. The little bit of light that does come through the windows from the outside floodlights casts long thin streaks of white on the cold stone floor. A chill races up Sister's Philomena's spine.

"Dear God, please help me find Delaney. Please do not let her be frightened. Keep her safe. Please don't let me panic!" prays Sister Philomena.

Arriving back at the courtyard where she and Capitano Leo agreed to meet, Sister still hasn't found Delaney. "Please, God," she prays intently.

"We have had no luck," says Capitano Leo when he

sees Sister Philomena. "How about you?" Then he sees
the fear in her eyes. "What? Have you seen a ghost?"

"Oh my, no. Even worse—I have lost sight of
Delaney," cries Sister Philomena. "She is somewhere in
this huge palace. Help me find her, please!"

Riley feels a lump in his throat and his stomach
turns inside out. "What do we do? How will we find
her? She'll be so scared!" Riley pleads.

"Can Bosco find her?" Riley searches Capitano
Leo's face for the answer.

"It is certainly worth a try," says Capitano Leo.

The captain takes a hold of the dog's ears and stares
directly into his eyes. "Bosco, find Delaney. Go, boy,
find Delaney."

The dog looks at Capitano Leo, then Riley, pauses,
and then puts his nose to the ground and sniffs. The
dog looks up, and starts to follow the scent of Delaney
back through section of the palace where Sister
Philomena and Delaney were searching. Bosco leads
the way through the now almost pitch-dark corridors
and rooms of the Popes' Palace.

Bosco stops in his tracks with his ears standing
straight up when he hears the sound of voices—voices
that do not belong to his master and his friends. Bosco
quietly sniffs the air, lets out a faint whine, but
remains perfectly still.

Capitano Leo can see the dim outline of the dog across the room and immediately senses that Bosco has stumbled onto something unexpected. If Bosco had found Delaney, the dog would be with her and moving excitedly by now—sniffing and licking. But the dog is as still as a statue, and that tells the captain that something is wrong, very wrong. Even brave Capitano Leo's heart is racing now. He puts up his hand as a silent signal for Sister Philomena and Riley to stop.

The three of them stand motionless, and in the quiet, they too hear the voices. Not loud, but definitely voices—maybe a man's and woman's.

Peeking through a doorway, Capitano Leo sees the glare of a flashlight and can make out the figures of two people in a room several doors away. The couple appears to be looking at a paper—it even looks like it could be a map of sorts.

Capitano Leo searches the darkness between him and Bosco and the people with the map. He squints. He can barely make it out, but he thinks he can see the outline of Delaney crouching behind a marble statue beside the doorway. As his eyes adjust to the dark, he is sure that it is Delaney. Thank God. But now he must figure out how to get her out of there safely.

Delaney has her back to Capitano Leo and Bosco and is trying hard to see what the couple is doing.

Bosco lets out another little whine. Then a low growl. Delaney turns, and looks right at the dog.

"Please, God, don't let those people harm her," Capitano Leo prays to himself.

Just then, Delaney puts her finger to her lips as if to tell Bosco to "Shush, be quiet."

Very carefully and quietly, Delaney crawls on her hands and knees back through the empty room, through the stone doorway, and into the safe arms of Capitano Leo. Bosco sniffs her hair, and if a dog can smile, he's smiling. She's safe! The Capitano puts his hand over Delaney's mouth just to remind her to keep quiet, and then takes her and Bosco back to where Sister Philomena and Riley are waiting.

When they are far enough away that they know the two people in the other room can't hear them, Sister Philomena asks her niece if she could tell what the man and the woman were doing.

"Aunt Philomena! I think they're the same people that Riley and I saw arguing in the train station in Siena, and at the Palio. She called him an *idiota*! I think the man was at Saint Catherine's house, too—only he was dressed as the fake nun," says Delaney.

"Are you sure?" questions Sister Philomena. She knows that Delaney pays attention and remembers even small details very well, and Sister trusts her to tell the truth. "That person we ran into at Saint Catherine's cell was dressed as a nun, so we thought it was a woman. Are you sure it was a man?"

"I'm sure now," says Delaney. "Remember that the nun's face had whiskers, like daddies have whiskers. That man back there in the room, he's got whiskers too, and it's the same face. Besides, there's a nun's habit on the floor under some brown wrapping paper. We saw this couple fighting over a brown package at the Palio. I think the package had the nun's habit in it."

"Very good! You are so smart, Delaney. Can you tell me what they were talking about?" asks Sister Philomena.

"No. They were talking in different languages. I couldn't understand what they were saying. Sometimes they talked in Italian, but not always. Sometimes they talked more from here," says Delaney, putting two fingers alongside her nose.

"I bet one was speaking Italian and the other French," concludes Capitano Leo. "This *signorina* is very observant with her eyes and her ears!"

"The man had a piece of paper with a drawing on it, just like the one the people had at the train station," Delaney continues. "The man would hold it one way and start jabbering. Then the woman would take it and turn it another way, push it in his face, and scold the man. I heard the woman call the man *idiota*—just like she did at the train station."

"Wow! You think the people we watched at the train station just happen to be the same people who were in Saint Catherine's house and are also involved with the ransom of Saint Catherine's letter?" wonders Riley. "We were that close to crooks and didn't even know it."

"You children are incredible," says a smiling Sister Philomena. "I didn't even know about the people in the train station. But I would not have suspected them of a crime at that time anyway. This teaches us that we always have to be observant of our surroundings."

"Capitano Leo, are we prepared to apprehend these crooks tonight?"

"It's possible." He hesitates, and then smiles coyly. "However, I might suggest waiting for daylight—let's let these two spend a scary night in this dark and creepy palace. From what Delaney tells us, they apparently cannot figure out "up" from "down" on their map—which is good for us. I doubt that either one is familiar with the Palace and its layout. Let them wander around in here in the dark all night. Besides, we should find the other half of the letter before they do, so that we can put it safely away and put a stop to any further ransom threats.

"Sister Philomena, I will call my associate in Avignon and arrange to have guards stationed at all the palace exits this evening," says Capitano Leo. "Just in case these two do find a way out, with or without the letter, they will be stopped. The guards will call us if this happens."

"Good," says Sister Philomena. "Let's get out of here. Capitano Leo, do you have a place for us to stay tonight?"

"I do," says Capitano Leo. "My associate, Andre, has arranged for us to stay on the other side of the river in a guest villa. The property is kept as a 'safe house' for visiting dignitaries and the operators will provide us with something to eat. After dinner we can plan our course of action for tomorrow."

CHAPTER ELEVEN

SCENT OF EVIL

Under the safety of darkness, Andre escorts this unlikely team of investigators first by motorboat and then by private car to the guest villa on the other side of the Rhône River. Even through the darkness, Riley can see that the villa is surrounded by beautiful gardens and is encircled by a low white stone wall. From the villa's terrace, he can see across the river. The Popes' Palace, the Cathedral of Our Lady of the Dome, and the Saint Benezet Bridge are lit with floodlights and look like something out of a fairy tale.

"I bet that if we had binoculars we would be able to see the crooks' flashlights flickering as they search inside the Popes' Palace," suggests Riley.

"Perhaps we could, but then we would stay up all night, just like the crooks," warns Sister Philomena. "Better if we rest and start fresh in the morning. We should begin our search at daybreak. We need to be out of the palace before the tourists begin arriving around 9 o'clock. Besides, the special guards will be on duty all night so if the crooks try to leave the palace they will be stopped."

Riley and Delaney are surprised by the food that is served in the guest house this evening, because it's terrific.

Their first course had been a slice of something that their aunt called pâté. She said it was made from the meat of a duck liver and was very popular in France. Riley was skeptical at first, but he spread some of it onto a piece of crusty bread and took a bite, and it actually tasted really good.

For the second course they were served big green salads with tomatoes, goat cheese melted onto crusts of bread, black olives, and cucumber slices. It was all very tasty so far.

But the main course is what brought the house down!

"It's French fries!" sings a delighted Delaney. "I love French fries. We never get them in the convent! I haven't had French fries since we left home."

Riley, with eyes as big as saucers and grinning ear to ear, looks at Sister Philomena for an explanation.

"Naturally, it's French fries. After all, we are in France!" Sister Philomena laughs quietly at the children's joy over such a simple food. "But they don't call them French fries here! They are *pommes frites.*"

By daybreak Riley and Delaney are up and dressed and ready to join the search of the Popes' Palace. They must find the missing half of Saint Catherine's letter.

"How come this letter is so important?" Riley asks Sister Philomena. "You said she wrote hundreds of letters."

"Indeed she did," explains Sister Philomena. "Saint Catherine is well known for her letters. There are 373 of her letters in existence—and this one would be number 374. Scholars have often thought there should be another letter, one that she may have written to Pope Gregory XI to commend him for his courage in returning to Rome to take back the Chair of Peter.

"Her letters are like words of love from God—they proclaim, among other things, love, truth, virtue, and wisdom in simple, easy-to-understand language. She had the gift of being able to take very complicated matters and explain them simply and logically."

"Are you two going to talk all morning, or are we going to search the Palace of the Popes?" interrupts Capitano Leo. "Our car has arrived and Delaney and Bosco are waiting."

The Popes' Palace looks even bigger and more forboding in the early morning light. What a monumental task they have before them!

"I had an idea last night," says Riley. "Why don't we use Bosco to find the letter?"

"He would have to have a scent of it first," says Capitano Leo. "How would we get the smell for him to search?"

"Wait!" says Delaney. "Don't we have one half? Can't he just sniff that?"

"Why yes, I still have the plastic bag from Saint Catherine's cell," recalls Sister Philomena. "I never had a chance to put it safely away, because we've been constantly moving about since we found it in Siena. I thought the safest place for it was right here inside my pocket." She hands the bag to Capitano Leo.

"It's worth a try," offers Capitano Leo.

He opens the bag up and holds it up to Bosco's nose.

"Bosco, *cercala!* Find this. *Vai. Via!!!*" commands Capitano Leo.

The dog just stares as his master as if to say, "You have to be kidding!"

"That won't work," reasons Capitano Leo. "It's just too big of a space to search, and too little scent. Besides, there are no footprints for him to follow like there were last night when he looked for Delaney."

Thinking it over for a minute, Capitano Leo has a possible solution. "Maybe the dog will be able to pick up the scent if we take him room to room and give him a sniff from the bag outside each room. However, we cannot leave it all up to Bosco. He is smart for a dog, but we need to continue to search too. We need to keep in mind that the likely hiding place is a loose floor or wall tile where the crooks could hide an object the size of this bag."

The search begins, floor-by-floor and room-by-room. Capitano Leo leads the dog to each room while Riley opens the bag to allow Bosco to get a whiff of the letter and note. Capitano Leo is concerned that there simply isn't enough material to give the dog a good scent to follow.

As they walk past one room, Bosco seems to hesitate but then continues on to the next room. But before they reach the next room, Bosco turns around, looks back to the room they just visited, and sits down. That's his signal that he's found something.

"Let's search that room more closely," says Sister Philomena. She is staring downward as she points her finger. "Check out this floor. It appears to be the original tile. It's the only room in the entire palace with anything original left in it. It was the popes' study. A likely place to search, wouldn't you agree?"

Sister Philomena, Capitano Leo, Riley, Delaney, and Bosco enter the study cautiously.

"Let's be extremely careful not to touch or damage any of the tile," warns Sister Philomena. "If you find any suspicious tiles, let me be the one to touch them. I have some gloves to protect my hands. We not only want to respect this historical building, but we also need to keep the surfaces free of our fingerprints."

Riley and Delaney tiptoe around the room.

Cautiously. Carefully. Curiously. Looking, but not touching.

"What about that one?" asks Delaney. The sun's rays are at such an angle that any unevenness in the tiles results in a thin shadow on the tile floor. Delaney resists a strong urge to touch the uneven tile, and waits for Sister Philomena. "Or that one?" she points. All of a sudden several of the tiles look uneven and loose.

"Good eye, Delaney," observes Sister Philomena. "Let me check them out."

Sister Philomena pulls on her gloves. She touches and then tries to wobble the tiles. First one, then another, and another. "A-ha!" she cries. She has found a loose tile, and wiggles it out of place. The tile comes up very easily, as if it had been recently disturbed.

"I think we have found it!" exclaims Sister Philomena, as she carefully removes a plastic bag from beneath the tile and turns it upside down to let the contents fall gently onto the floor. She is extremely careful not to get her fingerprints on it.

"Riley, hand me the bag from Siena, please." Sister Philomena briefly compares the contents of this bag to the contents of the bag found in Siena.

"That's it!" proclaims Sister Philomena. "It appears to be a match. Well done, team. The 374th letter from Catherine of Siena to Pope Gregory XI has been found. The Holy Father will be very happy."

"But wait!" An alarm bell goes off in Riley's head. "If we found the other half of the letter, it means the crooks did not find it. So where are the man and the woman we saw here yesterday?"

"The guards didn't see anyone leave the palace overnight, so they must still be inside the palace," says Sister Philomena.

"Capitano Leo, see if the officials would delay the opening of the palace to the public until we can search the palace for those two crooks. We can't put the lives of the tourists in danger."

"*Sì, sì, sorella.*" Capitano Leo picks up his phone and switches from Italian to French to speak to the person on the other end.

Now Riley feels like groaning rather than celebrating—they will have to do yet more searching. This whole situation seems even more dangerous to him now that they have both halves of the letter. "What if the crooks get really angry because we have it and try to take it away from us and hurt us? What if they have guns? What if there are more than two of them?"

Riley instinctively puts his arm around Delaney to protect his little sister.

"Good thinking," says Sister Philomena. "We will have to be extra cautious. But I think these must be pretty lame crooks if they were here all night and still didn't find the letter or find their way out."

"I know what to do," announces a confident Delaney.

The others look at her in disbelief.

"Let's go back to the room where I saw the man and the woman arguing last night. If Bosco gets their smell, maybe he can follow their footsteps and find them—like he found me!"

"Good idea," says Capitano Leo. "See how valuable my trusted dog, Bosco, can be. Now all we have to do is find our way back to that room."

"It's over here," Riley surprises them all with his ability to figure out where the room is located within the maze of rooms in the palace.

CHAPTER TWELVE

TRAPPED IN THE TOWER

Bosco takes up the scent of the crooks—up stone stairs, through room after room, down again, around and around. The crooks must have been wandering, lost, all night long.

Faster and faster—Bosco sniffs, switches back, sniffs, and then runs to the next room. Suddenly he runs through another door and into a long hallway. The two adults and two children struggle to keep up with him. The dog leads them up some more stairs, then out through a doorway, into the morning light, and onto a narrow catwalk that connects the palace with its watchtower.

The watchtower stands high above all the other parts of the palace, and even above all the other buildings in the city of Avignon. Riley imagines that this was the lookout where palace guards would stand watch, searching for invaders from across the river and countryside. How awesome is this!

Reaching the tower, Bosco ascends the narrow steps leading to the top. Gracefully, he leaps high in the air and lands on the floor of the high tower with four cut-out openings on each side. There, Bosco sits, growls, and then barks. He has found the crooks! The dog's bark grows louder and his tail begins to wag when he sees his master standing at the entry into the tower.

From the doorway, Capitano Leo can see a man and woman dressed in rumpled clothing and huddled together in the corner where they probably spent a good part of the night. They start to inch away further into the corner as Bosco continues to growl.

The man and woman are scrambling and pulling on each other as they attempt to stand up. They trip and stumble, trying desperately to keep away from the vicious-looking dog. Their eyes show panic as they realize that they are trapped. They have three choices: go past the barking and growling dog, jump off the tower to their deaths, or surrender.

"Buono. buono… Good dog, Bosco. Stand off!" commands Capitano Leo as he steps onto the tower floor.

Bosco lies down at the doorway but does not take his eyes off the would-be crooks.

The couple raise their hands up in surrender.

Capitano Leo frisks them and finds that they have no weapons, just a flashlight and a crumpled up, hand-scrawled map.

When Capitano Leo signals that it's safe for them to enter, Sister Philomena, Riley, and Delaney climb up into the tower. One of the crooks, the man who was dressed like a nun, recognizes Sister Philomena and the children. He begins to speak, but the wind blowing through the openings creates such a howl that no one can hear him.

Capitano Leo handcuffs the pair, helps them to stand up, and leads them through the door and back down the steep stairs. Sister Philomena, Riley, and Delaney follow. Bosco rides herd on the crooks while keeping a protective eye on his master, the nun, and the children.

"We can use the security guard's office to question these two," says Capitano Leo. "It was the base of operations for our special forces last night."

Sister Philomena questions the woman in Italian while Capitano Leo, who is fluent in both Italian and French, questions the man. The interrogations go on for nearly an hour. The crooks each tell their versions of the apparent break-in and ransom attempt.

Sister Philomena and Capitano Leo confer and then decide that the two stories match. They also conclude that the man and the woman are not skilled criminals but rather two poor, uneducated, and misguided people who thought they could take advantage of a situation.

"I am going to let the palace guards know it is okay to let the tourists into the Palace of the Popes now," announces Capitano Leo. "I am convinced there are no other people or crooks involved. Then I will explain everything to the Avignon police."

Capitano Leo calls the Avignon police and reviews the matter with them. The Avignon police are very cooperative and thankful for the assistance of the staff of the Vatican in this matter.

The police agree that they should take the two lawbreakers into custody because an apparent crime, a break-in at the Palace of the Popes, occurred in their jurisdiction. They tell Capitano Leo that they would gladly participate in a further investigation relating to the long-lost letter of Saint Catherine, but feel that Sister Philomena should return the letter to the Vatican for safekeeping. They tell her that if they need it as evidence, she can personally bring it back to Avignon.

"So tell us what happened!" Riley demands as Sister Philomena emerges from the security guard's office. Riley, Delaney, and Bosco have been waiting patiently in the adjacent courtyard for almost two hours. The children feel as if they're about to explode from the curiosity.

CHAPTER THIRTEEN

CRIMINAL INTENT

Sister Philomena sums up the case for Riley and Delaney.

"As I suspected, a letter—this letter," she holds up the two plastic bags, "was sent to Pope Gregory XI by Catherine of Siena when the Pope was still in Avignon.

"Unfortunately, by the time the letter arrived in Avignon, Pope Gregory was already on his way back to Rome. The mail was very slow in those days, as it had to be carried on foot or by horseback.

"In her letter, Catherine praised Gregory XI for having the courage to return the Papacy to Rome. However, the letter fell into the hands of the new occupant of the Popes' Palace. His name was Clement VII and, as Delaney would say, he was a fake pope. The letter never got forwarded to Pope Gregory XI, the real pope."

The kids both frown as they try to follow the details of what Sister Philomena is telling them.

"Okay. I'll review the history. You have to realize that this occurred in 1377, over 700 years ago. The

French Cardinals who surrounded Pope Gregory XI in Avignon at that time didn't want the Papacy to move back to Rome. They were afraid that the move would take power and influence away from them. They liked living in Avignon where they enjoyed rich food and drink and loads of luxuries, and seemed to ignore the needs of the faithful. There was no way they wanted to pack up and move to Rome along with Gregory XI. So, in an act of rebellion, the French Cardinals elected their own pope, and he called himself Pope Clement VII. The period in Church history when this happened is sometimes referred to as the 'Western Schism'. Later Church historians gave the French popes, the fake popes, the label of the 'antipope' or 'false pope'.

"So, Catherine's letter was delivered to Clement VII, the fake pope, and he must have opened and read it. As I said, the letter praises the real pope, Pope Gregory XI, for his courage. This must have made the fake pope, Clement VII, angry and jealous. It was no doubt out of jealousy that the fake pope decided not to forward it to Pope Gregory.

"However, Clement must have known the letter was important and valuable, so he decided just to preserve it rather than destroying it.

"Before Clement died, he gave this letter to his nephew, who in turn passed it on to his descendents. Catherine's letter to Gregory XI has been passed down from generation to generation for hundreds of years. Apparently it was mixed in with some old journals and no one ever paid any attention to it.

"According to the two people we caught, our so-called crooks, they just got the letter when someone in the family died. It was just by dumb luck that they discovered it in the journals and realized its importance."

"So how come the letter ended up in two places?" questions Riley.

"Well, the man and woman are cousins. One lives in Italy and the other in France. A childless uncle who was a remote descendent of Clement VII left the letter to both of them when he died. Apparently the man and the woman didn't really trust each other from the beginning. They tore this priceless letter in two, and each took a half. For safekeeping, the man hid his half in the Palace of the Popes in Avignon and the woman hid her half in Siena, in the Sanctuary of Saint Catherine.

"The man wanted to use the letter to extort a lot of money from our current pope and the Catholic Church, and he was trying to convince his cousin to go along with him. The woman wasn't sure what to do with the letter. Her husband wanted them to donate it to the Vatican Museums so all the world could see it.

She had a hard time making up her mind. However, in the end, the thought of getting some money for it was too tempting for the woman. Greed is an evil power.

"Without telling her husband, the woman decided to meet secretly with her cousin. They were to tell each other where the respective halves of the letter were hidden and go together to retrieve them.

"Big problems arose when they went to recover the halves of the letter from the hiding places. In order to go unnoticed, one of them had to dress as a nun to get back into the Sanctuary of Saint Catherine in Siena to collect the woman's half. Linking what the woman confessed to me and what you kids told me about the two people fighting over the package at the Palio, they were deciding who was going to dress up like a nun. The habit was in the package. Obviously, the man lost! Our paths crossed, big-time, when we were in Saint Catherine's cell and he came disguised as a nun to retrieve the letter.

"Another really big problem came about when the man could not find the room in the Popes' Palace where he hid his half of the letter."

"But he had the map, the *carta!*" recalls Riley.

"Yes, he did," smiles Capitano Leo. "But the man wasn't so smart. It appears that he drew the map after he hid the letter, on his way out of the Palace of the Popes. The problem is the map had no proper reference point; no north, south, east or west, no up or down. It started at 'X' and counted steps. However, since he didn't know which way was which when he put the 'X' on the map, and because the palace is so huge, he could not retrace his steps. That's why she kept calling him an '*idiota*.'"

"What happens to them now?" wonders Riley.

"As strange as it seems, there isn't much of a crime here at all. The intent was there, but they did not fol-

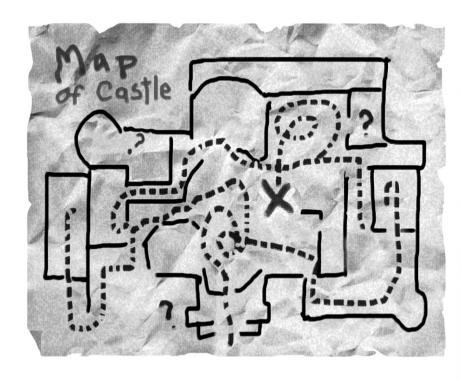

low through with the ransom demand, so they may be cleared of any actual wrongdoing," explains Capitano Leo.

"The two cousins inherited the letter, so they should have a right to possess it. On the other hand, the letter may legally belong to the heirs of Gregory XI. In that case, the cousins are in possession of stolen property. However, because they had no way to know it was stolen, there is no punishable crime. You could also argue that the letter rightfully belongs to the Vatican, because it was addressed and sent to Pope Gregory XI. I guess the real crime happened 700 years ago when Clement held on to the letter that was intended for the real pope. In today's law, a crime like that would be considered postal fraud, but I don't know if that existed 700 years ago. Anyway, that crime is way too old to prosecute."

"The bottom line is that we have recovered a treasure with tremendous historic value. The Avignon police may charge the cousins for breaking and entering, or loitering overnight in a public place, the Palace of the Popes.

"As an act of atonement, the lady definitely wants to give the letter to the Pope, as her husband suggested, and have it displayed in the Vatican Museums," adds Sister Philomena. "I am pretty sure her cousin will agree to her plan, particularly after all of this. I predict that the Pope will give them something as a reward and to thank them for their contribution, especially if they seem repentant. Too bad for them, the Pope probably would have given them a greater reward, praise, and recognition if they had just offered it when they received it from their uncle."

"Cool," is how Riley sums up his feelings.

"Good job, all of you," praises Capitano Leo. "You too, Bosco! Without you we would not have found Delaney or our thieves. Good dog!"

The dog licks his master's hand and wags his tail.

"Aunt Philomena, I'm hungry. Can we go and get something to eat?" asks Delaney.

"That sounds like a great idea," smiles Sister Philomena. "What do you say we go find some French fries!"

"Yeah! Yeah!" sing Riley and Delaney. "*Pommes frites! Pommes frites!*"

"And you too, Bosco? How about a great big dog biscuit?"

"Woof!"

$$= \text{THE END} =$$

ITALIAN AND FRENCH WORDS AND PHRASES LEARNED ON THIS ADVENTURE

*Le parole e le frasi italiane che abbiamo
imparato in questa avventura
(Italian)*

*Les mots et les expressions françaises que
nous avons apprises sur cette aventure
(French)*

Traveling to foreign places and meeting people from other countries is always exciting. Even if you travel only in your thoughts while reading about foreign places and people, the experience is still very exciting. Learning to communicate with people from other countries makes a trip that much more fun. Here are some English, Italian, and French words and phrases that Riley and Delaney would have learned in this adventure, *Secrets of Siena*.

Words and Phrases Found in this Adventure

English	*Italian*	*French*
Enough	basta	assez
Hello/goodbye	ciao/arrivederci	bonjour/au revoir
Come here!	vieni qui	tu viens ici
Please/thank you	prego/grazie	s'il vous plaît/merci
Palace	palazzo	palais
Good morning	buongiorno	bonjour
Good evening	buona sera	bonsoir
Would-be thief	ladro potenziale	voleur potentiel

Geographic Features

English	Italian	French
River	fiume	fleuve
Road	strada	route
Mountain	montagna	montagne
Valley	valle	vallée
Field	campo	zone
Stream	corrente	flot
Walkway	passaggio pedonale	passage couvert

Food and Beverages

English	Italian	French
Milk	latte	lait
Water	acqua	l'eau
Fruit juice	succo di frutta	jus de fruit
Scrambled eggs	uova scrambled	oeufs scrambled
Bacon	bacon	lard
Vegetables	verdure	legumes
Salad	insalata	salade
French fries	patate fritte	pommes frites

Animals

English	Italian	French
Horse	cavallo	cheval
Oxen	buoi	boeufs
Cow	mucca	vache
Sheep	pecore	moutons
Pig	maiale	porc
Dog	cane	chien
Cat	gatto	chat
Fish	pesci	poissons

Titles

English	Italian	French
Pope	Papa	Pape
Sister	sorella	soeur
Brother	fratello	frére
Captain	capitano	capitaine
Mister	signor	monsieur
Madame	signora	madame
Train conductor	conduttore di treno	conducteur de train
Friend	amico	ami
Police chief	capo di polizia	chef de police
King	re	roi
Queen	regina	reine

Other Adventures with Sister Philomena,
Special Agent to the Pope, include:

LOST IN PETER'S TOMB
Book #1. Riley and Delaney arrive in Italy to spend the summer with their aunt, Sister Philomena. Riley is not at all happy about living in the convent. That changes when Sister Philomena rushes them to the Vatican to help the Pope find an intruder in the Apostolic Palace.

BREAK-IN AT THE BASILICA
Book #2. A poor man hides in the Basilica of Saint Francis in Assisi in the dark of night as he plots to steal something of value. Once the crime is committed, Sister Philomena, accompanied by her niece and nephew, is sent to investigate. A mysterious wolf keeps appearing!

CURSE OF THE COINS
Book #3. The 30 pieces of silver that Judas was paid for betraying Jesus are found in Israel and sent to the Vatican. But then they disappear! The Pope asks Sister Philomena to find them, which takes her, Riley and Delaney on a fast-paced, often dangerous, race through Rome and its numerous basilicas.